MONSTER and CHIPS

Food
Fright

For Helen, Robert, Sam and Ben

Big monstery thanks to the audience at the Edinburgh International Book Festival 2013 who helped to create the monster Sluggybottom Ninjapants in Chapter Four.

I'd like to acknowledge all the hard work of the people who have made Monster & Chips so much fun to create, in particular Harriet, Sam, Lily, Elorine, Kate and Matt.

MONSTER and CHIPS

Food
Fright

BRAINS!

Written and illustrated by
DAVID O'CONNELL

HarperCollins *Children's Books*

www.monsterandchips.com

CONTENTS

First published in Great Britain by HarperCollins *Children's Books* 2014
HarperCollins *Children's Books* is a division of HarperCollins*Publishers* Ltd,
77-85 Fulham Palace Road, Hammersmith, London W6 8JB

Visit us on the web at
www.harpercollins.co.uk
www.monsterandchips.com

1

MONSTER AND CHIPS - Food Fright
Text & Illustrations copyright © David O'Connell 2014

David O'Connell asserts the moral right to be identified
as the author and illustrator of this work.

ISBN 978-0-00-749719-5

Printed and bound in England by
Clays Ltd, St Ives plc

Prologue

Did you know that there are places where our ordinary world rubs against strange, magical worlds? When this happens holes sometimes get worn between the two, creating doorways.

It can happen anywhere.
Perhaps on a street near you.
An ordinary-looking door will
appear, so ordinary that you might not
even notice it. Like the door of a diner –
just a place that sells burgers and chips.
But there might be a very special diner
on the other side of that door, with very
special customers...

CHAPTER 1

Terror of the Towering Sandwiches

Joe Shoe was bored. It was quite possibly the longest school day of his entire life. His teacher, Mrs Sprattly, was going for the world record in how-many-dull-subjects-can-you-talk-about-without-taking-a-breath. It was looking like she had a good chance of beating the previous record holder (also Mrs Sprattly) by some way. Her current subject was

sock-making in the Himalayas. To relieve the

boredom, school bully Grotty Grace was casually

flicking the back of Joe's head with a rubber band.

"I'm just softening your head up for the thumping you'll get later, you little bum-toot," she growled over Joe's shoulder.

Joe didn't bother to argue. It would be like trying to reason with a Snappish Grumpmonster, and Joe had met enough of those to know better. Joe had met a lot of strange

creatures at Fuzzby's Diner. Fuzzby's was a café for hungry monsters and it served the best chips ANYWHERE.

Joe had discovered the monster diner hidden down a spooky alley, behind a magic door. It was owned by Fuzzby Bixington, a big green friendly monster who had offered Joe a job. Joe helped to serve the monster customers and cook the disgusting food they loved to eat. He was the only 'hooman' as they called him who had ever found the diner, and he'd been having loads of adventures with Fuzzby and his monster friends ever since.

BBBBRRRIIIIIIIIIINNNNNNGG! Much to Joe's

relief, the school bell rang. He quickly dodged Grace's fat hands as she tried to grab him, and rushed out of the school gates.

I bet Fuzzby never got the back of his head flicked by a rubber band, thought Joe as he ran down the alley to the familiar red door of Fuzzby's Diner with its bright neon sign. But when the door opened, it wasn't Fuzzby who greeted him, but a large, furry YELLOW monster, with one big eye and a pair of horns.

"Hello, Joe!" it said cheerily, just like Fuzzby normally did. Was Fuzzby wearing a costume, dressing up as another monster?

Joe was confused until a green furry face

appeared over the other monster's shoulder,

grinning happily. It was the real Fuzzby, in his

striped apron, waving a spatula dripping with

bubbling brown grease.

"Hello, Joe!" he said. "I see you've met my

cousin, Zuffby. He's here for a visit."

The diner wasn't too busy, so Joe and Zuffby sat down at one of the tables while Fuzzby continued cooking. They sat next to the Guzzelins, a family of little rock monsters who were regulars at Fuzzby's. The Guzzelins were slurping their favourite pongleberry and gurglefish milkshake and giggling whenever little Lemmy Guzzelin burped purple bubbles from drinking too quickly.

"I've heard all about you, Joe," said Zuffby with the same cheery grin as his cousin. "Fuzzby tells me you're the key ingredient for the smooth

running of the diner."

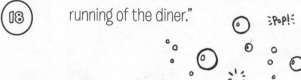

"After me, of course!" came a gruff voice.
A four-eyed creature with tentacles slithered
on to the chair next to Joe. It was Barry, the
diner's cat. He didn't look like a cat, but no
one was going to argue with Barry as he liked
arguing and was very good at it.

"I taught Joe everything he knows," Barry said importantly, and gave Joe a look that dared him to say otherwise.

"Maybe you can teach Fuzzby a thing or two about cooking," said Zuffby with a wink (or possibly a blink - it was difficult to tell when a monster only had one eye). Fuzzby pretended to look cross for a second, then they both roared with laughter.

Joe glanced up at the day's specials

displayed on a board on the wall:

Joe didn't think that Fuzzby needed any

lessons in how to cook, especially if you liked

to eat things that came out of jars labelled

REVOLTING, EXTRA-HAIRY and POSSIBLY POISONOUS.

"Do you cook as well?" asked Joe.

"We're all cooks in the Bixington family,"

WILFRED BIXINGTON

ZUFFBY'S FIRST
SANDWICH
(SNEEZE & PICKLE)

MADAME
FILOU'S
SCHOOL OF COOKING

FUZZBY
BIXINGTON
HAS PASSED HIS
EXAMINATION IN
CHIPS

GREAT UNCLE MARCEL

COUSIN DELILAH

explained Fuzzby. "Zuffby runs a sandwich shop in Monsterworld."

"Zuffby's Mega-Monster Sandwich Emporium, to be precise," the big yellow monster said proudly. "There's nothing that goes on between two slices of bread that I don't know about. Though my favourite sandwich is the BLT."

"Bacon, lettuce and tomato?" said Joe, surprised. Monsters didn't normally go in for 'hooman' food.

"No, bogslime, lice and toadwart," said Zuffby. "With the crusts cut off to make them nice and posh. I'm also quite partial to sneeze and pickle, spawn mayonnaise and pee-not butter and jelly. I know all the special sandwich fillings, from ant-berry to zog brains."

MUNCH
MUNCH

"BRAIINSS!" said Cuthbert, a zombie cupcake that lived in a little cage on the counter. Joe had created him accidentally one afternoon by sprinkling zombie powder over some cupcakes. Cuthbert's five little eyes blinked brightly at the mention of brains. They were his favourite food. Fuzzby fed him scrambled eggs and pretended they were brains, but Cuthbert didn't seem to notice and mostly sat happily in his cage.

Joe saw that Barry had a mischievous look on his face.

"I'll bet you can't make a sandwich as good as Fuzzby," the cat said to Zuffby innocently.

Uh-oh, there'll be trouble... thought Joe.

The two monster cousins eyed each other.

"I bet I can," said Zuffby, holding Fuzzby's stare.

"I bet I can make the biggest, most spectacular mega-monster sandwich ever seen since the Great Fish Paste Catastrophe at last year's Monster Fair!" said Zuffby loudly.

The customers in the diner gasped and dropped their cutlery in shock.

"What happened at the Great Fish Paste Catastrophe?" whispered Joe.

"Boris Swampot made a sandwich so big that even Mr Jubbins couldn't finish it," said Fuzzby. Mr Jubbins was a blue jelly monster who often came into the diner. Mr Jubbins's huge see-through tummy was legendary – it could take ANYTHING, and sometimes did.

Fuzzby continued the tale. "He ate so much rancid fish paste his insides began to bubble and blow up like a balloon, until soon he was bigger than a house. But he couldn't keep all that gas inside for ever. Before long he let out a fart so big and loud that it blew away half the fair and set fire to the rest, as well as sending a shock wave that shattered

windows in the nearest town. And he was

followed around by hundreds of cats for days

afterwards."

"Us cats like a bit of fish, you know," Barry pointed out helpfully, as Mr Jubbins shifted uncomfortably in his chair.

"Think you're up to the competition, Fuzzby?" said Zuffby, coolly examining his nails.

"Of course!" said Fuzzby, slamming a fist on the countertop. "A Bixington never backs away from a challenge. Let the sandwich contest begin!"

The customers all cheered and eagerly gathered round the two big monsters. If there was going to be a food battle between two of the best cooks in Monsterworld, then they wanted to see it, especially if there was a chance of some free grub.

Fuzzby got straight down to business.

"Joe, you can be my helper," he said. "And Barry can help Zuffby. First sandwich to reach the ceiling wins round one. Then – the tasting round!"

"Gentlemen, choose your weapons!" said Barry, bringing the bread bin in from the kitchen and setting it down in front of the monsters. Fuzzby quickly picked some crusty scab bread loaves and Zuffby grabbed some beetle wholemeal bread.

"It has better strength for heavier fillings," he boasted.

Those beetles do get between the teeth, though!

"You have to think of these things if you're trying out a serious bit of bread engineering. Plus the beetle leg bits are nice and crunchy."

The two monsters stacked up their slices of bread on the counter next to a large tub of eel-grease butter. Grabbing a spreading knife each in their claws, they waited for the signal to start.

The Guzzelins provided the countdown. "Three... two... one... GO!!" they squealed.

With a flash of blades, Fuzzby and Zuffby

set to work, buttering the first slice of bread.

"Get me spider pickle!" called Zuffby,

sending Barry slithering off to the store

cupboard.

"Frog-egg jam!" shouted Fuzzby, and Joe ran to grab a jar of the green-blue preserve from the fridge. He gave the jar to Fuzzby just as

Barry handed Zuffby the tin of gooey pickle.

The monsters grabbed the fillings and slapped them on to their waiting buttered bread, spreading them haphazardly so that they slopped over the edges of the crusts. Then they each threw another slice of bread on top, squidging the filling a bit more. The first layers were done.

"Plug-hair relish!" shouted Fuzzby, and Joe

ran over to the cupboard.

"Dribblefruit chutney!" shouted Zuffby

at the same time, and off Barry went to the

kitchen shelves.

 "Stinky-rat cheese!"

shouted Fuzzby.

"Nosewart ketchup!"

shouted Zuffby.

 "Crabspit sausage!"

shouted Fuzzby.

"Itchy-bum nettles!"

shouted Zuffby.

 BRAIINSS! said Cuthbert,

who was feeling left out.

The monsters continued to call out ingredients for their sandwiches, while Joe and Barry went back and forth to the kitchen like two yo-yos. As soon as they arrived back at the counter, Fuzzby and Zuffby grabbed the new filling, hastily added an extra layer to their sandwiches and shouted for the next. The customers cheered as the sandwiches began to grow taller and taller. Some monsters even started to take sides, cheering on their favourite sandwich.

Then, just as Joe was running back from the fridge with a bowl balanced in each hand, Barry accidentally on purpose stuck out one

long tentacle. It wrapped round Joe's ankle and
the food went flying, both bowls skipping along
the counter and knocking Cuthbert's cage over.
The little cupcake bounced around inside it.

"Hey!" shouted Joe crossly.

"Well, you should watch where you're going!" said Barry, smiling slyly.

Joe righted the little zombie cupcake's cage. "Sorry, Cuthbert," he said, before dashing off to fetch some fresh ingredients.

Soon the sandwiches were taller than even the two monsters could reach.

"Surely they'll have to stop now," wheezed Barry, out of breath from all the toing and froing. "My tentacles can't take any more!"

The monsters didn't look like they were

stopping, however. Zuffby was in his element

as an experienced sandwich maker, but Fuzzby wasn't put off by his cousin's advantage. He loved anything to do with making food, and always put his heart and soul (and a few other bits and bobs) into his cooking.

The sandwiches were now so tall that Fuzzby and Zuffby had to spread the fillings on to slices of bread then throw them on to the top of their sandwich towers, like soggy Frisbees. Soon the two cousins had recruited the Guzzelins into the competition, giving them the fillings in little pots and hurling them on to the top of the stacked sandwich layers.

screamed the Guzzelins as they soared upwards. Then, once they had landed, they quickly spread the fillings before jumping off and being caught on the other side by the whooping customers.

The Guzzelins loved extreme sports, especially if they involved something yummy, and they giggled hysterically the whole time. Lemmy Guzzelin even did a midair somersault for the entertainment of the audience. Unfortunately the Guzzelins' aim didn't always match their enthusiasm, and sometimes a filling would miss the sandwich completely and go flying across the diner. This made all the monsters roar even more, especially when one splatted someone in the face.

"We're neck and neck!" exclaimed Fuzzby. "The sandwiches are almost at the ceiling!"

There was only enough space for one more filling. Fuzzby was just that bit quicker. He threw Lemmy and his pot of zitberry jam high over the tower of bread. Unfortunately, Fuzzby threw the little Guzzelin far too hard and with a THOMP! the rock creature smashed through the ceiling, leaving a small, Lemmy-shaped hole. A moment later, Lemmy's face peeped out from behind the broken plaster.

SORRY, MR. BIXINGTON!

"Never mind, Lemmy," said Fuzzby good-naturedly, even cheering with everyone else when Zuffby tossed the final slice of bread into the air. It just skimmed the ceiling and landed neatly on the top of his sandwich.

"I win this round!" said Zuffby, grinning broadly.

"He'd be nothing without me," said Barry, relishing his triumph over Joe. "One-nil to the cat, hooman."

But Fuzzby wasn't ready to admit defeat.

"It's time for round two," he said. "As we all know, you can't judge a sandwich on size alone."

"True," agreed Zuffby. "Everybody tuck in!"

The monsters all cheered and began to devour the delicious sandwiches, pushing each other out of the way to get to the tastiest bits. One scaly lizard creature used its long, forked tongue to lick a dollop of dribblefruit chutney from over the heads of the monsters in front.

MUNCH! MUNCH!

A family of fly monsters buzzed round the tower of food, taking bites as they circled it, making the fillings splurt and gloop everywhere. Claws swiped. Mouths chomped. The sandwiches wobbled and swayed as they were attacked from all sides.

In the middle of all the mess and merriment, Joe suddenly noticed that Cuthbert's cage door was open. And the cage was worryingly empty of a small, five-eyed, sharp-toothed and dangerous cupcake.

"Barry!" Joe shouted over the noise of munching monsters. "Cuthbert's missing!"

"He must be somewhere," said Barry. "How

far can a small bit of sponge-cake travel?"

Joe and Barry looked around them. There was so much mess it would be difficult to find a little cupcake. Where could he have got to? Joe had once been trapped in a room full of zombie cupcakes and had only just escaped with his brain in one piece. Cuthbert might only be one little cake, but he could get up to all kinds of mischief!

"Cuthbert!" Joe called, looking under the tables.

"BRAIINSS!" came the muffled reply. It seemed to be coming from above.

"Cuthbert?" said Joe again.

"BRAAIINS!" came the reply again. Joe couldn't quite work out where it was coming from, but it sounded a little closer this time.

Joe watched as the monsters continued to eat, the sandwiches slowly losing height.

Then a horrible thought occurred to him.

"Barry," he said, "didn't Zuffby use scrambled pterodactyl eggs as one of his fillings?"

"Oh yes," said Barry. "There was a big bowl of it in the fridge. He's used it in several layers of his sandwich."

"What's up, Joe?" asked Fuzzby.

"It's Cuthbert!" whispered Joe. "He's not in his cage!"

"What's that?" said Fuzzby, who couldn't hear him above all the noise and excitement.

Joe watched uneasily as the monsters kept eating and the sandwiches lost another layer.

"I think Cuthbert might have fallen into the bowl of scrambled pterodactyl eggs and ended up inside one of the sandwiches!" said Joe a bit louder. But still Fuzzby couldn't hear.

Zuffby looked up from the crowd of hungry monsters, his mouth covered in crumbs and nosewart ketchup. "Does this mean I have to stop

eating my beautiful sandwich?" he said, dismayed.

"Only the layers that have scrambled eggs in them," explained Joe. "And we have to stop everyone else eating them too!"

"What's going on, Joe?" said Fuzzby, coming over at last. He could see that the hooman looked worried.

"Cuthbert's got out of his cage and I think he's in Zuffby's sandwich, about to get eaten!"

"WHAT?" said Fuzzby.

"Mr Jubbins has already eaten one of the egg layers!" squeaked Lemmy Guzzelin, jumping up and down.

They all rushed over to where the jelly monster was still chewing on a crust of bread.

Fuzzby picked him up and peered inside his see-through belly, giving him a shake so that the contents of his giant tummy swirled around. Mr Jubbins burped loudly in astonishment.

"No sign of Cuthbert here," said Fuzzby, plonking Mr Jubbins back down again with such a bump that a surprised fart rippled across his big blue bottom. "Unless he's already been digested."

"Cuthbert?" yelled Joe desperately.

"BRAIINS!" came a very muffled reply.

"It's coming from above! He's still in the sandwich!" Joe shouted with relief. But the monsters hadn't stopped eating and the

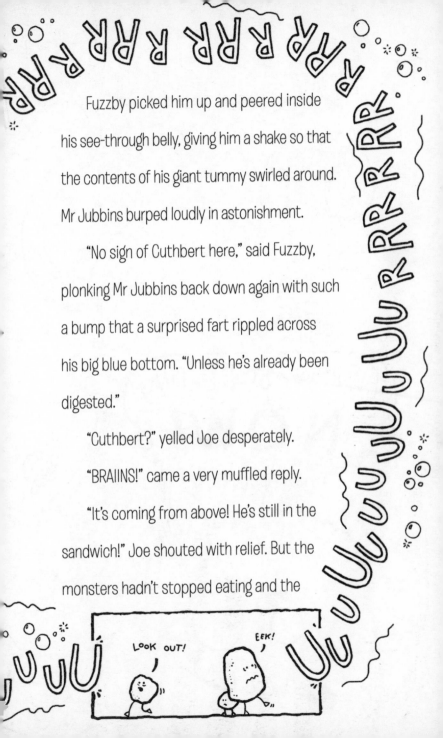

sandwiches were getting smaller by the second. It wouldn't be long before Cuthbert met a grisly fate between some monster's jaws!

"BRAAIIINS!" Cuthbert's voice was getting closer and closer as the sandwich towers began to descend.

EVERYBODY STOP EATING NOW!

shouted Fuzzby.

The monsters all looked up, surprised and disappointed.

Joe and Fuzzby frantically began pulling apart layers of bread and filling from the sandwiches.

Suddenly, Joe spotted a little leg hanging out from between two slices of bread, high up on Zuffby's sandwich.

"I can see him!" Joe shouted to Fuzzby. He pointed to the wriggling leg.

"I can just about reach..." said Fuzzby, making a grab at the sandwich. But it was too much for the tower of food.

It rocked. It shook.

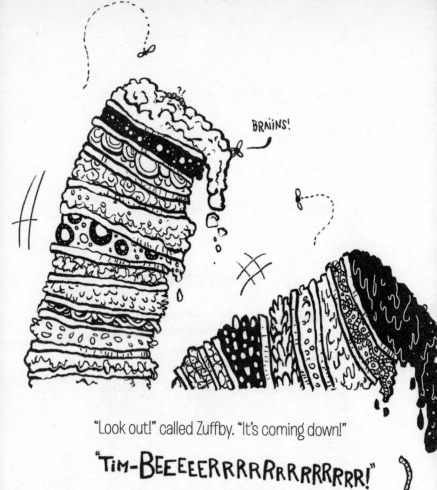

BRAiiNS!

"Look out!" called Zuffby. "It's coming down!"

"TiM-BEEEEERRRRRRRRRRRRRR!"

cried Fuzzby, as the column of bread and filling

collapsed, colliding with Fuzzby's sandwich on

the way past.

Oh No!

Poor old Cuthbert!

As the two towers fell, the monsters were buried under a giant avalanche of bread and fillings. On the top sat a little zombie cupcake, its five eyes blinking through a covering of scrambled egg.

oops!

Zuffby's furry face emerged from underneath the mess. He flicked some chutney from his nose.

"That was a very fine sandwich," he said. Then after a moment, "Yours was too."

Fuzzby grinned. "Delicious. Both of them."

"Shall we call it a draw?" said Zuffby.

"Good idea," agreed Fuzzby. "How did you know Cuthbert was in the sandwich, Joe?"

"Oh, I just had a brainwave," said Joe. "Isn't that right, Cuthbert?"

BRAIINSS!

said Cuthbert happily.

CHAPTER 2

Sunken Secret
of the Sink

The diner was in more chaos than usual. Firstly,

the brand-new dishwasher had broken down

and Fuzzby had almost run out of clean plates.

The dirty ones were stacked up in greasy piles,

stuck together with cold, leftover food.

"I only got the dishwasher last week," said

Fuzzby. "And my boiled-sprout-and-sickpea dip

has been the most popular special today. It

doubles up as cement for filling cracks in the walls, so it's going to be tough getting those plates apart."

Joe checked out the day's specials on the board on the wall:

TODAY'S SPECIALS
Boiled-Sprout-AND-Sickpea Dip AND CHiPS
Wriggling Ravioli AND CHiPS
Pilchard Pudding with Frog Custard AND CHiPS
RiBBiT!
oink!
Warthog Whisker Biscuits AND CHiPS
Barf Brownies AND CHiPS
Spicy Clumps of Something AND CHiPS
PLEASE DO NOT EAT THE SPECIALS BOARD
Pustule Soup AND CHiPS
POOT!
FUZZBY'S
TRY OUR FAMOUS CHIPS!
BUT WHAT DO WE EAT OFF?

Joe didn't fancy getting too close to any of them.

But dirty dishes weren't the only thing troubling Fuzzby.

"We've got a thief!" announced the big green monster as he walked into the café from the kitchen. "Never, in all the days since I opened the diner, have I known anybody to steal my food!"

Joe was shocked. He'd met the odd monster who wasn't so nice, but mostly monsters were a friendly, honest bunch. They weren't the kind of creatures who went around stealing.

"What did they take?" asked Gordon, a red insect monster who was one of Fuzzby's regulars. He was slurping the remains of the pilchard pudding from his plate, having dissolved it into a soup using a spurt of his acid saliva.

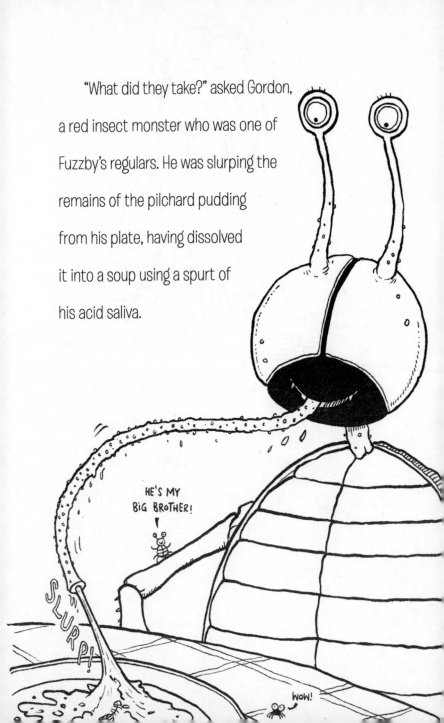

HE'S MY BIG BROTHER!

SLURP!

WOW!

"Not your oil-slick salad with the seagull dressing?" gasped Doreen, an ancient sea monster, and another of Fuzzby's regulars. "I simply couldn't bear it if you ran out of that!" She gave a horrified shiver that sent a cluster of barnacles clattering to the floor.

"They've taken some food from the store cupboard," said Fuzzby. "I found the door open this morning and there was a box of lice crispies missing. It was definitely there yesterday. Barry doesn't like them so I can't blame him this time."

"Me-oow!" said Barry with an offended sniff. "I don't steal food! I might allow myself a tiny morsel every now and again, but that's a perk of being the diner's cat, you know!"

"Who would want to steal food from here?" asked Joe, astounded. Then he quickly corrected himself. "Er... I mean, it's delicious and everything, but it seems like such a mean

We're on the trail...

thing to do."

"Aqua-mice," said Barry.

"What?"

"Aqua-mice!" repeated Barry. "I'm sure it's them, the little blighters!"

"Aqua-mice?" said Joe. "What are you talking about?"

"Mice who live underwater, of course!" said Barry. "Aqua-mice! Little devils with their snorkels and flippers and secret undersea hideouts! Don't you get them in hooman world? Either it's aqua-mice, or someone's had

a widdle in the kitchen. There was a big pool of water by the open store-room door this morning. It's the only explanation."

"Well, while you're playing detective," said Fuzzby with a sigh, "somebody has to get on with the washing-up. Sorry, Joe, but I'm going to have to put you on sink duty today. I'm too busy cooking to help, I'm afraid."

Joe groaned. "On my own?" he said. Washing-up was never fun, whether you were in a monster diner or not. He looked at the piles of dirty dishes. Some of them looked back at him menacingly.

Just then, the diner
door opened and Twig
appeared, smiling happily. She
was a little tree monster who often went with
Joe and the others on adventures.

"Hello, everyone!" she called.

"I think we may have found a volunteer to
help you," said Fuzzby with a wink at Joe.

Luckily, Twig was more than happy to help
out. She didn't mind washing-up and enjoyed
spending time with Joe and hearing his stories
about hooman world.

"Let's get the plates stacked up and into

the kitchen," she said eagerly. "Then we can fill

the sink with bubbles and get washing!" She was a little too keen for Joe's liking, but the sooner they got started, the quicker they'd have the job out of the way.

They managed to get the dirty dishes into the kitchen without too many breakages and piled them all up next to the sink.

Joe was just telling Twig about the thief, the puddle by the cupboard door and the aqua-mice when they heard something.

GRRRROOOWWWWWWL

"What was that?" he said. "It sounded like it was coming from the sink."

"It didn't sound much like a mouse..." said Twig.

The sink was made for Fuzzby and was extra-large-monster-sized. It was so huge that

Joe could easily have taken a bath in it. He and

Twig needed to stand on chairs just to peek

over the side and look in.

"There it is again! It's coming from the plughole..." said Joe. He pulled himself over the edge and eased himself down the sink's slippery side. Twig clambered after him. They carefully leant over the plughole and peered into its shadowy well.

"The thief must have come up through here," said Joe. "But it's too small for anything to fit."

"It's big enough for mice," said Twig, leaning against the tap. As she did so there was a click, and suddenly the plughole opened out into a wide entrance, easily big enough for a hooman to get through.

"It's a secret door!" exclaimed Joe. "Maybe
it's a door into Monsterworld." Joe knew there
were such things hidden all over the place.

"We should tell Fuzzby!" said Twig. But when she tried to clamber out of the sink, her root-like feet slipped against its smooth side. She slid backwards, knocking into Joe like a bowling ball. Joe lost his balance too and a second later they were both falling down the plughole!

They shot along the dark pipe beneath the sink as if it were a slide, rolling round and round and down at a terrifying pace. The pair were soaking wet and covered in bits of smelly, leftover food.

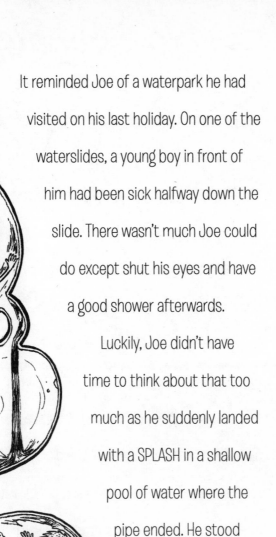

It reminded Joe of a waterpark he had visited on his last holiday. On one of the waterslides, a young boy in front of him had been sick halfway down the slide. There wasn't much Joe could do except shut his eyes and have a good shower afterwards.

Luckily, Joe didn't have time to think about that too much as he suddenly landed with a SPLASH in a shallow pool of water where the pipe ended. He stood up slowly, then was

WAY OUT

knocked over almost immediately as Twig

flopped out of the pipe after him and collided

with the back of his head.

"Ouch!" said Joe crossly, getting up again.

"Sorry!" said Twig. "That was fun, wasn't it!"

"I suppose so," said Joe, who was a bit less

convinced.

They got up and looked around. It was

mostly dark, but spots of daylight streamed

in from somewhere high above their heads,

allowing them to see through the gloom. They

were standing ankle-deep in a stream of water

in a long tunnel. It was crisscrossed by other

tunnels that headed away into darkness. In

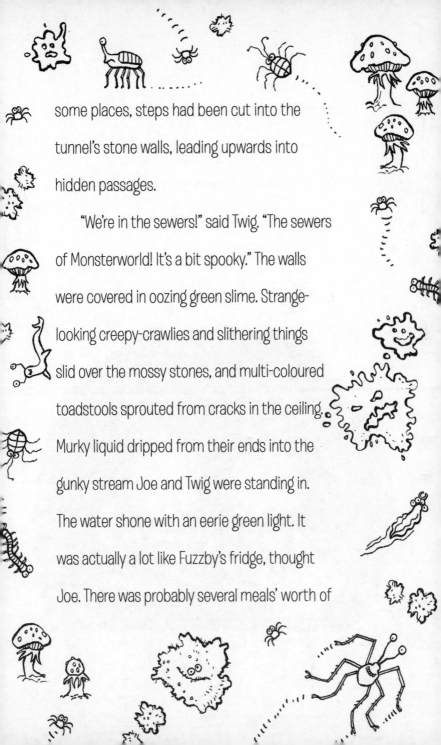

some places, steps had been cut into the

tunnel's stone walls, leading upwards into

hidden passages.

"We're in the sewers!" said Twig. "The sewers

of Monsterworld! It's a bit spooky." The walls

were covered in oozing green slime. Strange-

looking creepy-crawlies and slithering things

slid over the mossy stones, and multi-coloured

toadstools sprouted from cracks in the ceiling.

Murky liquid dripped from their ends into the

gunky stream Joe and Twig were standing in.

The water shone with an eerie green light. It

was actually a lot like Fuzzby's fridge, thought

Joe. There was probably several meals' worth of

monster food hanging off these walls.

Just then, a pair of eyes surfaced from the stream in front of them and blinked. Joe and Twig jumped backwards in surprise.

"Afternoon!" burbled a voice from an unseen mouth. The eyes were attached to a fish monster that spouted sewer water from the blowhole on top of its head. Using its fins and snake-like tail, it wriggled up the wall of the tunnel. "Visiting relatives, are you?" it said chattily, waving a fin and blinking constantly. "We don't get many tourists down here."

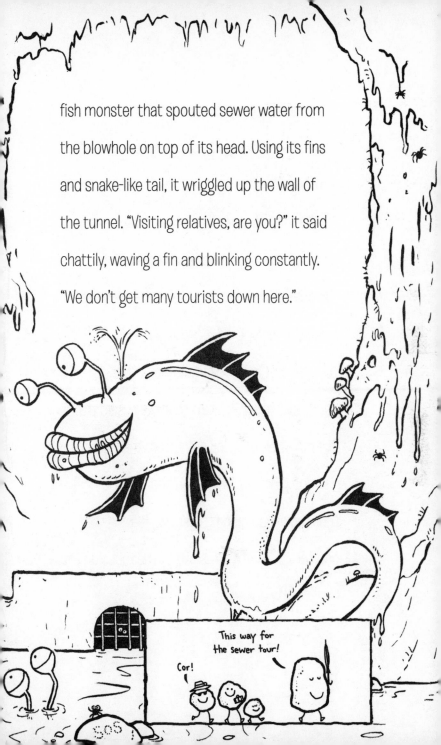

This way for the sewer tour!

Cor!

SOS

"We're on the trail of a thief," said Joe. "Have you seen anyone? Or heard any strange growling?"

"Oh, the Growler," said the creature, hanging from the wall at eye level with Joe. "No one's seen it yet, but we've all heard the noises," it whispered.

Joe and Twig looked at each other.

"Last I heard, it went thataway," said the fish monster, pointing a fin down the tunnel.

Joe grabbed Twig's arm and the two of them splashed along the sewer, leaving the creature picking worms out of the moss on the wall with a hooked tongue.

Ahead they could see the tunnel disappear round a corner. Light from above bounced off the murky green water at their feet, creating strange spooky patterns on the walls.

"What's that?" gasped Twig. A large shape moved sluggishly in the dim light in front of them. It was only a shadow, but whatever had made it was close by. Joe dragged Twig to the side of the tunnel where they flattened their backs against the wall to stay hidden. The shadow slowly grew smaller as whatever it was moved further away.

GRRRROoooooooooo ooooooooooo echoed along the sewer.

"It's the thief! And it's definitely not a mouse..." whispered Joe. "Let's follow it and see where it goes."

As quietly as they could, they edged around the corner. There was nothing to be seen, but they could still hear the GRRRROOOWWWWWWL from the darkness ahead.

"You don't want to go down there," said a voice above them. They looked up and saw a cluster of mega-slugs curled round a mushroom on the ceiling. Slime dripped from the creatures' giant, glistening bodies on to Joe and Twig's heads. The slugs took drooling bites out of the fungus, chewing it into a frothy

pulp. "Our friend Mortimer went down there last week and never came back," said one of the mega-slugs darkly.

"Mortimer was a bit like that, though," admitted another, its stalky eyes examining them closely. "Always longing for excitement, always wanting the fast life. I knew he would have a sticky end."

"We're mega-slugs!" the first mega-slug said, wiggling its tail so that slime dripped off it and fell into the sewer water with a SPLAT! "We always have sticky ends!" They chuckled at the joke. Joe sighed. They really didn't have time for mega-slug comedians.

"We're looking for a thief," he said. "We think it came down here. It growls a lot."

"The Growler? Rather you than us! It went

thataway..." said the mega-slugs, pointing their tails down the tunnel. "But don't say we didn't warn you."

Twig was getting nervous. She trembled so that leaves began to fall from her branches and were carried off on the stream.

"I don't like the sound of this," she said miserably as they plodded through the sewer. "I thought we were looking for a cute little mouse, all soft and squeaky. But this monster sounds big and scary."

"Well, I guess we'll find out in a minute. I think whatever it is, it should be just round this bend..." But when they turned the corner there was nothing there. No shadows, no growling. No aqua-mice.

"Great. Nothing. And now we're lost!" said Twig. "How are we going to find our way back to the diner?"

"Can I help?" said a small soggy voice.

Joe and Twig looked down. In front of them stood a little smiling monster, holding a box and slowly chewing like a cow. She had

grey skin that shone as if it was wet.

"I'm Dungbelle," said the monster soggily.
"I'm a drain-troll. Are you lost? I don't get
many visitors down here. A mega-slug passed
through last week but he didn't stay long. Not
even time for a cup of tea!"

Twig let out a deep sigh of relief. "We've been looking for a thief," she said. "A terrible growling monster!"

"No terrible growling monsters here," said Dungbelle. "I would have heard them."

"Oh dear," said Joe. "What shall we do now?"

"You could try a bit further on," said Dungbelle helpfully. She pointed down the tunnel. "I've heard there's a bog shark living down there. But mind the overhead pipe. That's where the diner toilets empty out. You could end up with a brown hairdo if you're not careful."

Joe and Twig thanked her and were
just about to head down the tunnel when
they heard the enormous

GRRROooooooooooo oooooooooo ooo oo oo

again. But there was only Dungbelle standing in
front of them.

"Oooh, excuse me!" she said.

Joe and Twig looked at each other.

"Was that your tummy making that noise?"
asked Joe.

"Beg your pardon," said Dungbelle,
embarrassed. "I've been ever so hungry, you

see. My stomach's been making all kinds of
funny noises."

"What's in that box?" he asked.

"Just some nibbles," said the drain-troll
innocently.

"Are they lice crispies, by any chance?"
said Joe.

The monster was about to protest, but the
game was up. She let out a huge sigh.

"You've caught me!" said Dungbelle
miserably. "Ever since Him Upstairs got himself
a fancy dishwasher, there haven't been any
food leftovers coming down the pipes from
the sink any more. I like leftovers the best –

they're all squidgy and cold."

Suddenly it all started to make sense.

"So you came through the secret door in the plughole and took Fuzzby's lice crispies," Joe said, pointing at the box the monster was holding.

"Do you think Fuzzby will be angry with me?" asked Dungbelle.

"Not if you can show us the way out," said Joe thoughtfully. "And I might even be able to help you find some food..."

"It's this way," said the drain-troll, looking much happier as she led them towards another side tunnel. Suddenly she shrieked

and pulled them to one side, out of the

stream, as a group of small creatures with

snorkels and flippers sped past. "Aqua-mice!"

she whispered. "Watch out for them. Highly

dangerous!"

Fuzzby was standing outside the diner looking

puzzled. Joe and Twig had disappeared. He

peered down the alleyway. Had Joe gone home

already? They hadn't even started the washing-

up. That didn't matter now, as Fuzzby had managed to fix the dishwasher and he'd soon have some clean plates to use. But he was still worried.

Suddenly, there was a noise from somewhere near his feet. With a loud clatter a manhole cover in the alley was pushed up and slid aside. A familiar scruffy head popped up from the hole.

"Joe!" said Fuzzby. "Where have you been?"

"We've caught your thief," said Joe, jumping up from the drain, followed by Twig and a nervous Dungbelle. "But she has a good excuse."

Joe explained what had happened. As he expected, Fuzzby wasn't angry, just glad to see them safe and well.

"But what about Dungbelle?" said the big green monster, scratching his head. "We can't have her going hungry."

"Your dishwasher is huge," said Joe. "And Dungbelle likes living in the wet. Maybe she can live inside the dishwasher? It'd be like her own Jacuzzi – a Jacuzzi that comes with a food

supply. Then you wouldn't have to worry about

the pipes getting clogged up with leftovers."

Dungbelle and Fuzzby were both delighted

with the arrangement.

"Let's shake claws on it, Dungbelle," said

Fuzzby, grinning. "Welcome to the diner! We'll

have to introduce you to the regulars, and

Barry. Where is Barry?"

Just then, the diner door opened and Barry appeared, dripping with water and staggering about dramatically. There were cookie crumbs all over his face.

"It's the aqua-mice, Fuzzby!" said the cat. "They've struck again! They found the piranha cookies... I tried to stop them, but there were just too many! I think they might have stolen

The cat is a rat!   Bad kitty!

a few frog-custard doughnuts as well. And

maybe some dribble cake. That was very tasty.

Probably. I wouldn't know, of course. Er... why

are you all looking at me like that?"

CHAPTER 3

The Great Brutish Bake-off

It was strangely quiet in the diner. For a moment, Joe couldn't work out what was wrong.

Was there someone missing? There was Fuzzby, busy behind the counter. There was Dungbelle, happily asleep inside the dishwasher. There was Cuthbert in his cage, staring at a dish of cabbage jelly.

"BRAAIINS?" said Cuthbert hopefully.

There were all the customers happily

tucking into their food. Bradwell was sitting

at his usual table, tackling some particularly

complicated knitting while trying to eat a bowl

of wiggling worm noodles. The noodles were wiggling out of the bowl, getting tangled up in the wool. They were dangerously close to being knitted into a giant sock (Bradwell had very large feet). That will make the sock very tickly, thought Joe, but at least Bradwell can have a snack later when he takes it off, with some extra cheesiness if he's lucky.

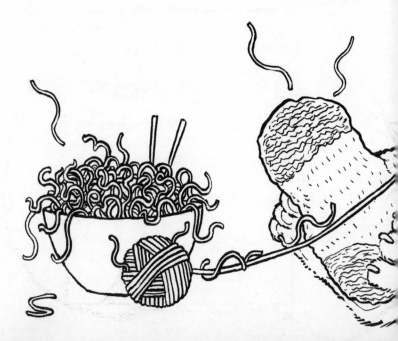

The Guzzelins were also in for the afternoon, and were chomping their way through a many-layered sandwich. They had developed a taste for sandwiches since Fuzzby and Zuffby's competition, and were happily munching on this specially made one. It had each of the day's specials as a separate filling:

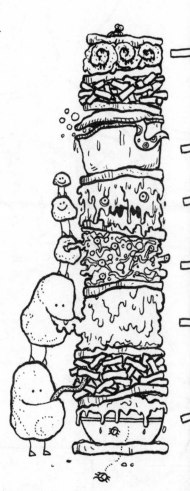

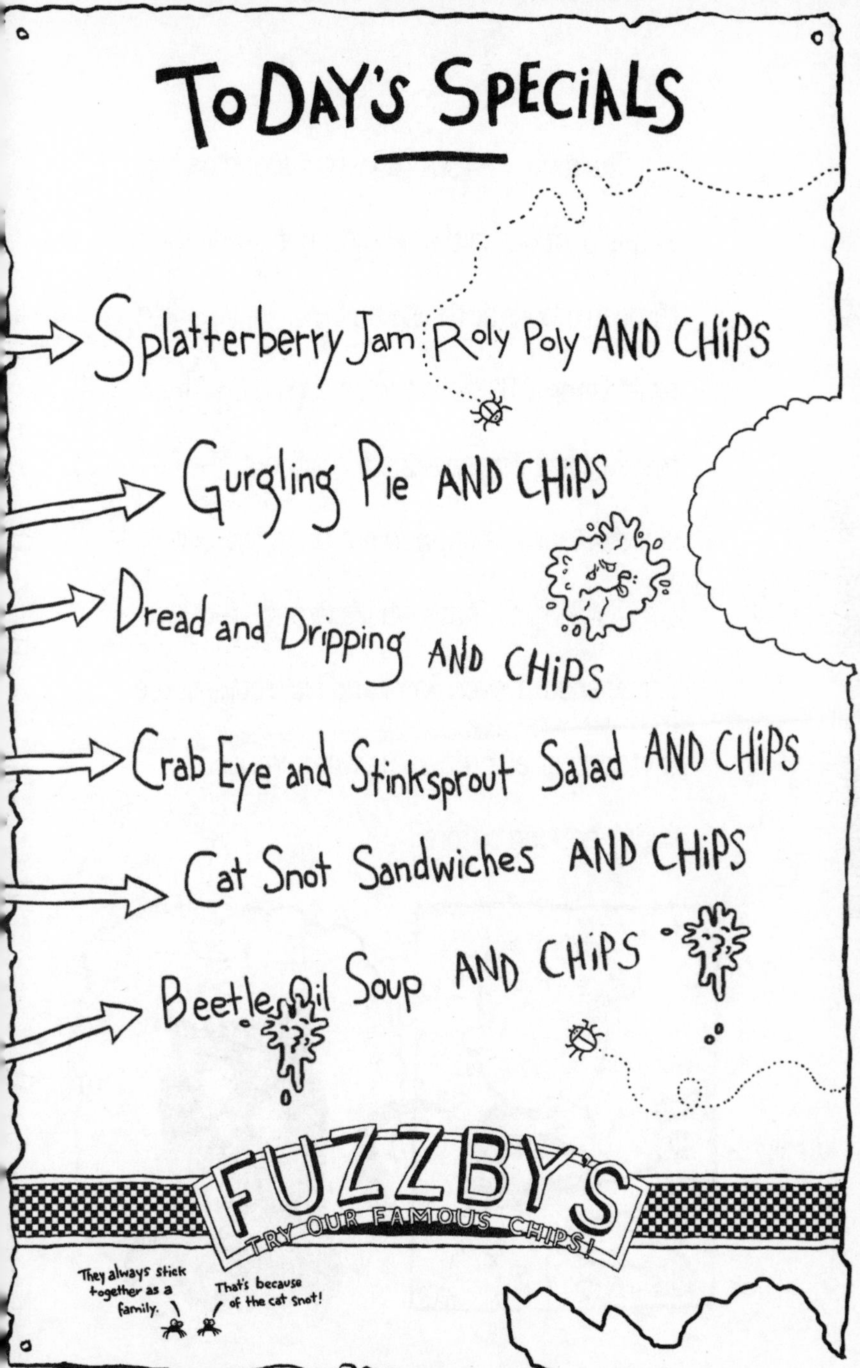

ToDay's Specials

→ Splatterberry Jam Roly Poly AND CHIPS

→ Gurgling Pie AND CHIPS

→ Dread and Dripping AND CHIPS

→ Crab Eye and Stinksprout Salad AND CHIPS

→ Cat Snot Sandwiches AND CHIPS

→ Beetle Oil Soup AND CHIPS

FUZZBY'S
TRY OUR FAMOUS CHIPS!

They always stick together as a family.

That's because of the cat snot!

The family of rock monsters stood on top of one another so that they could all chew through a layer at the same time. They giggled when Lemmy Guzzelin took a huge mouthful, making the filling splodge messily out of the sides. A tentacle flopped out on to the plate.

TENTACLES! That's what's wrong... thought Joe. He hadn't seen Barry and his troublesome tentacles all afternoon. He was surprised he hadn't noticed before.

"Where's Barry?" Joe asked Fuzzby.

The big green monster grinned wickedly. "Come to the workshop and have a look," he said. Fuzzby led Joe into the kitchen. There at the back of the room was a door with a sign on it that said **WORKSHOP** Joe knew that doors had a habit of appearing in the diner whenever they were needed. He'd seen this one before.

"This is where the Fuzzbuggy is kept!" said Joe excitedly. They stepped into the workshop and there stood the enormous yellow van. The Fuzzbuggy was a mobile diner with a kitchen built into it and a hatch in the side to

serve customers through. Joe had been on

adventures in the Fuzzbuggy before and hoped

they were about to go on another one.

Barry was sullenly polishing its hubcaps.

"Finished!" said the cat to Fuzzby with a

flick of the washcloth. "Look how clean that is!"

"You've done a good job," said Fuzzby as he carefully inspected the paintwork.

"Good job? I can see my face in it!" said Barry. "And a very handsome chap I am too," he purred to himself, smoothing his whiskers.

"I told Barry to give the Fuzzbuggy a good clean," said Fuzzby to Joe. "It's his punishment for pinching the piranha cookies and blaming the aqua-mice."

Barry sniffed resentfully. "No one could have cleaned it as well as me, anyway," he said. "And you wouldn't want it to look dirty for our outing."

"Are we taking the Fuzzbuggy on a

We helped!

trip?" asked Joe eagerly. "Are we going to

Monsterworld again?"

"Yes, we are!" said Fuzzby. He handed Joe

a black envelope. "Look, this monster mail

arrived this morning."

Monster mails were talking letters that

the monsters sent to each other when there

was important news. This one was asleep, little

papery snores fluttering up from its mouth-

flap. Joe gave it a gentle shake.

"Oi!" it said, yawning. "I gave

you the message, didn't I?"

"I wasn't here," said Joe.

The monster mail sighed.

"Dear Mr Bixington," it began with another yawn, "you are invited to take part in this year's Monster Fair. The fair is expecting many visitors who will all want feeding. With your reputation for good cooking, you will be a welcome addition to the various rides and attractions. Yours monstrously, the Monster Fair Committee. End of message. Can I go back to sleep now? I've had a very busy couple of days."

"What's the Monster Fair?" asked Joe excitedly.

"The Monster Fair is a wonderful day out. All the monsters in Monsterworld come. They have a huge fairground with rides, food, music and other entertainment. It's a great honour to be asked to provide the food. It'll be good for business," said Fuzzby enthusiastically. "And we'll get to have a bit of fun too. The fair is this weekend, though, so we'll have to get cracking with the cooking!"

They went back to the kitchen where Fuzzby pulled a large, heavily stained and slightly burnt book of recipes off the shelf. He flicked through the pages with his sharp claws, then tore out the pages for the recipes he liked.

"I think we'll have burgers..." he said as several sheets of paper sailed out of the book. "Maybe some cookies... hot dogs... a bit of salad... Variety is the key, of course..."

More pages flew from the book. Joe gathered them from the floor and studied the recipes. They were going to need lots of ingredients. He made a list of the things he wanted, then rummaged through the store cupboard until he had found everything.

Barry scoffed. "I don't need to look at

a recipe to know what I'm doing," he said. "Cooking is an art and I am an artist! A dash of this, a sprinkle of that, a splodge of the other and voilà! That's French for 'Barry is a genius'."

Joe rolled his eyes. This was going to be hard work.

"In that case, genius," Fuzzy said, "you can get started on making a batch of cookies. We're going to need loads."

"Easy," said Barry breezily. "Now... er, what do I do first?"

Joe sighed and handed him the recipe.

They were soon busily mixing and stirring, chopping and slicing, or in Barry's case hammering, picking bits off the floor and scowling.

It wasn't long before a huge spread of different snacks and other food for the fair were covering the kitchen table. There were mini scab-burger bites, little pots of dead-and-buttered pudding and kebabs of octopus

GROOWLL!

tentacle in maggot sauce. Lastly, there was a large grump-cabbage all ready to be cut up and made into a salad. It was sulking and muttering to itself in the middle of the table.

"There'll be chips to go with it all, of course," said Fuzzby as he surveyed the feast happily.

Joe had just finished making some weevil and bumbean chilli in a big saucepan. The brown goo was burping and bubbling nicely. Joe had learnt quite a lot in his time at the diner and Fuzzby had even said he'd make quite a good cook, though Joe couldn't imagine monster food going down well at home.

"How are you getting on?" Joe asked Barry.

"Just putting the finishing touches to these cookies," said Barry with pride. "I think you'll agree that they're the best cookies you've seen in a while. They're cat-cookies, in fact." Barry had decorated all the cookies with little Barry-like cat faces. He'd even made mini tentacles for them out of liquorice worms. Joe

had to admit they did look all right, but it was

a bit alarming to be surrounded by so many

Barrys. They all seemed to be grinning at him in

a cheeky Barry kind of way too.

Fuzzby came over from the cooker to have a look. He had been cooking some sausages that were sizzling away in a frying pan. Even he was impressed by the cat-cookies.

"Well done, both of you!" he said. "Now, let's think about– Hang on a minute! Did that cookie just stick its tongue out at me?"

"Don't be daft!" said Barry. "You must be working too hard, Fuzzby. You're seeing things." The cat turned to look at his biscuit creations. "Hmmm. I'm sure there were more of them here a second ago."

Just then Bradwell appeared at the counter.

"Have you seen my ball of wool?" asked the monster. "I had it on the table... and then it disappeared. It can't have walked off by itself!"

At that moment, a ball of wool wandered across the counter in front of Bradwell's surprised face.

"But then I could be wrong, of course," he said quickly.

"Meow," said a squeaky little voice. A small round head appeared from behind the wool.

"It's one of the cat-cookies!" said Joe.

"Look, there are more of them!" said Bradwell. A couple of the miniature Barrys were tangled up in his noodle knitting, unravelling

I think it's time to leave...

the giant sock as they played with the wool.

"Meow!" they squeaked happily.

"Barry, what did you put in your cookies?"

asked Fuzzy sternly.

"I did exactly what the recipe said," replied

Barry innocently. "Almost."

"Did you make zombie cookies?" asked Joe.

"BRAAIINS!" said Cuthbert appreciatively. Joe remembered when Cuthbert had been brought to life after zombie powder was accidentally sprinkled over a batch of cupcakes. Joe and Twig had been trapped in the kitchen for ages.

"I didn't make zombie cookies!" said Barry. "Fuzzby got rid of the zombie powder after what happened last time."

The other cookies began to get restless, shifting about the table in a sly, cat-like way.

"You must have done something," said

MEOW!

Fuzzby. "Cookies don't just come to life of their own accord."

"I may have made a few minor improvements," admitted Barry, "like adding a dash of Bake 'n' Wake so they'd rise a bit better." He held up a packet to show them.

"Barry!" said Fuzzby, sounding quite cross. "Bake 'n' Wake isn't for helping things rise – it makes things come to life! I add a tiny bit to my pies so that they can tell me when they've finished cooking... but only ever a pinch."

"Oh dear," said Barry with a nervous gulp, giving the obviously empty packet a shake. "I added a bit more than a pinch."

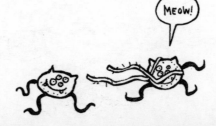

MEOW!

"Meow!"

They turned round to see the cat-cookies making a run for it. Just like cats, they were quick in their movements, darting across the table to avoid being caught. They meowed constantly.

"And I thought one Barry was bad enough!" muttered Joe as a little cookie slithered through his fingers.

"Oi!" said Barry. "Mind how you handle my cookies!"

"What can we do, Fuzzby?" asked Joe.

"Eventually the Bake 'n' Wake will wear off," said Fuzzby, "but we have to round up those

cookies immediately or they will pass on its effects to the other food too. It's extremely catching!"

As if in answer, a growl came from the cooker, shortly followed by a... "Woof!"

"What was that?" said Joe as a sausage appeared over the edge of the frying pan. The sausage was growling. It sounded very cross about something.

"Oh no!" said Fuzzby. "The hot dogs must have been infected by the Bake 'n' Wake! And they have a spicy flavouring that makes them particularly bad-tempered. Not to mention the fact that they hate cats!"

"Uh-oh, they've spotted the cat-cookies..." said Joe. "I don't like the look of this!"

Sure enough, the hot dogs had hopped out of the frying pan and were chasing the hissing cat-cookies round the kitchen, leaving little greasy trails behind them. Joe tried to pick one up, but quickly dropped it.

"OW!" he yelled, "they're hot!"

The cat-cookies panicked, scampering in all directions on their little tentacles as the hot dogs slid after them, covering the floor in a slick of oil, yelping and growling the whole time. They even tried to chase Barry, sending him darting up on to a shelf for safety. Joe couldn't

help laughing at the cat-monster trembling in fear at the sight of a ferocious sausage.

"Look at this mess, Barry!" bellowed Fuzzby. The big green monster tried to grab the hot dogs, but with a "YIKES!" he skidded on the greasy floor, knocking over a table of food that had been made for the fair and sending it all flying. Fuzzby landed with a CRASH! as the snacks rained down around him.

"Shut that door, Joe!" yelled Fuzzby. But it was too late. The cat-cookies dashed across the kitchen floor and into the diner, the hot dogs sliding after them, barking with excitement.

Just when I thought
I'd seen everything...

They swept around the feet of the customers (those that had feet), sending monsters tripping over each other and bumping into chairs and tables. Plates of food and cups of sludge-tea plunged to the floor, adding to the mess and muddle.

"Oh no, the Bake 'n' Wake will get into everything now!" groaned Fuzzby. "We'll have a full-scale food fight on our paws if we're not careful!"

No sooner had he uttered the words, then the scab-burger bites bounced into the diner, little bits of scab flaking off with every tiny leap. They jumped on to the customers' tables and hopped across the startled monsters'

plates. Living up to their name, they chomped great big bites out of everyone's food as they passed.

"Oi!" shouted a furry grumblebeast whose Gurgling Pie had been nibbled by a burger bite. "Get off my pie!"

WHO SAID I WAS YOUR PIE?

gurgled the pie, to the surprise of the grumblebeast.

The food on the plates was coming
to life as the effects of the Bake 'n' Wake
took hold! Customers discovered their
dinner looking back at them and grinning,
or escaping off the plate. A monster that
looked like a giant crab with pointy legs
and a scaly tail desperately tried to catch a
pile of glueberry pancakes that were sliding
about the table, but they dodged every
snap of its pincers and left a sticky trail of
syrup over everything. One of Twig's tree
monster friends found its mud pie pudding
clambering into its branches and refusing to

move. Then a family of smoke bats quickly

moved in and made

a nest out of it.

A monster that looked like a cross between

an ostrich and a hippo was chased round

the table by his own cat-snot sandwich. It

snapped its bready mouth viciously at the

monster, spraying snot, fur and feathers all

over the place.

A herd of twittering peas swept the Guzzelins
from one side of the table to the other and
back (which the Guzzelins enjoyed immensely).

And through the middle of all this chaos raced
the cat-cookies and hot dogs, meowing and
barking furiously.

"Don't be alarmed!" cried Fuzzby heroically. "Everything's under control. Sort of."

Meanwhile, back in the kitchen Joe stood ankle-deep in noisy snacks, unable to move as the food swarmed around him. Barry was still stuck up on the shelf, cornered by a pack of hot dogs.

"Fuzzby!" Joe yelled. "We have to do something. These hot dogs are dangerous!"

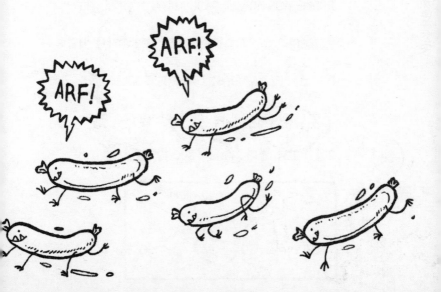

Fuzzby ran in and grabbed a spatula, skilfully steering some of the hot dogs back into the frying pan, where they panted happily from all the excitement.

"They're the least of our worries," shouted Fuzzby. "If the Bake 'n' Wake gets into your weevil and bumbean chilli, we're in real troub–"

"Uh-oh," said Barry from the shelf. They all looked at the big pot of bubbling chilli. A cat-cookie was tiptoeing round the edge of the saucepan, swaying like a tightrope walker in the breeze. Fuzzby edged towards it carefully.

"Gently... gently..." he said. He reached

out a claw and made a sudden grab at the

cookie, but it ducked,

quivering dangerously.

For a moment it kept

its balance, then with a

MEOW! its tentacles lost their footing and the

cat-cookie toppled into the boiling chilli with a

great big

"Oh no..." said Fuzzby.

The chilli began to froth and bubble violently as the Bake 'n' Wake took effect. Gooey tendrils of brown rose above the rim of the pot, growing slowly bigger and bigger. A small mountain of chilli was now bubbling up, standing high over the cooker and smoking dangerously.

"Stand back, everyone!" warned Fuzzy.

"What's happening?" said Joe, backing away fearfully.

"Bumbean volcano!" said Fuzzby. "Chilli and Bake 'n' Wake are a very dangerous mix..."

The chilli volcano trembled and the

saucepan rattled on the stove-top. The kitchen

shook as the volcano growled threateningly.

The cat-cookies scattered in every direction, squeaking in terror. Joe and Fuzzby hid behind the door, while up on the shelf Barry found refuge inside the piranha-cookie jar. The sides of the volcano suddenly ballooned outwards, wider and wider, as if it was taking a gigantic breath. It growled more and more loudly, and shuddered and shook until all of a sudden...

There was a sound like a wet fart as the

volcano collapsed in on itself, shrinking back

into the now-silent saucepan.

They all looked at Fuzzby.

"Phew! The Bake 'n' Wake has worn off!" he said. "Panic over, everyone!"

And sure enough, just like that, calm returned to the diner, the cat-cookies stopped their meowing and the burger bites would bite no more. But there was a terrible mess and a lot of unhappy customers.

Fuzzy looked at Barry.

"I was only trying to help!" whined Barry, before anyone could even start blaming him. "I thought my attempt at cooking went rather well. I think I have a natural talent for it,

actually. Perhaps I should try something more ambitious next time."

"Why don't you try cleaning up this mess first," said Fuzzby, looking at the devastation. He threw a mop in the cat's direction. "You probably have a natural talent for that too," he said with a grin. "Perhaps you could give us a demonstration?"

CHAPTER 4

The
Monster Fair

AWoooGAH!

It was a sound Joe recognised instantly.

The Fuzzbuggy's noisy horn:

AWoooGAH!

Joe rushed to his bedroom window. There

was the big yellow van parked outside his

house, with Fuzzby, Barry and Twig sitting up

front in their 'hooman' disguises of sunglasses

♫ We're all going on a summer holiday... ♫

and terrible fake beards. Fuzzby waved at Joe

from the driving seat.

They were off to the Monster Fair!

Joe had never been to the Monster Fair

before, but he'd visited Monsterworld a few

times. It was a strange place, full of strange

creatures, hidden from our 'hooman' world

behind secret Gates.

Joe dashed downstairs excitedly and clambered into the van.

"Let's go!" said Fuzzby. He started up the van's engine and with an **AWOOOGAH!** the Fuzzbuggy roared away down the street.

"Hello, Joe," said Twig. "It's going to be such an exciting day! I'm really looking forward to having a go on all the rides. And look at all this food!"

The van was filled with all the food that Joe, Fuzzby and Barry had made that week. Joe could hardly see from one end of the Fuzzbuggy to the other. They'd even brought Barry's troublesome cat-cookies, thankfully no longer meowing. And Joe was glad to see the

Fuzzbuggy had its own specials board. It was

just like being in the diner:

"We'll soon be there!" said Fuzzby as he turned the Fuzzbuggy down a side street. The road ran alongside a railway viaduct. Joe remembered that there was a Gate into Monsterworld somewhere near here. And sure enough, when they got to the seventh arch of the viaduct, Fuzzby drove the van into its dark interior and pressed a button on the dashboard labelled GATE.

The ground beneath them rumbled and trembled, but the Fuzzbuggy pushed on through the darkness before suddenly bursting out into daylight again. They were in Monsterworld!

The Fuzzbuggy trundled down a busy road. There were lots of monsters in their cars all going in the same direction.

ARE WE THERE YET?

"Are they all going to the Monster Fair?" asked Joe.

"Oh yes," said Twig, taking off her beard and glasses. "It's one of the busiest days of the Monsterworld social season. Anybody who is anybody will be there!"

"And anybody who is nobody too!" added Fuzzby. "And they'll all be hungry." He grinned in anticipation.

The road led to an enormous field that was packed with multicoloured tents and huge, sweeping fairground rides. A giant banner with **MONSTER FAIR** written on it flapped overhead in the breeze. The place was filled with noise –

music, laughter and happy monster voices all mixed together in one big hullaballoo.

Joe read the signs for the rides as they drove through the field. There was the **BIG GRIPPER**, a huge roller coaster that zoomed round a looping track while the screaming monsters clung on for dear life (it had no seats). There was a **HAIRY-GO-ROUND** where you could have a ride on the back of a yeti, or if the yeti was in a bad mood then it would have a ride on your back. Then there was the **BIG SQUEAL**, a Ferris wheel that spun faster and faster until you were sick, which was a bit unfortunate if you happened to be standing underneath it. Monsters have a strange idea of fun, thought Joe.

The music was just as odd. On a stage, a band of young monsters were playing bizarre instruments that looked like they had been made out of the leftovers from an explosion in a drainpipe factory, and were producing a sound like an elephant with digestive problems. Monsters of all shapes and sizes were merrily hopping and dancing around in time to the noise.

"It's the Furry Things," said Twig, admiring the young monsters with a dreamy sigh. "They're the most popular band in Monsterworld."

And then there were the smells. Joe was used to the less pleasant side of hanging out with monsters (especially monsters who actually had their sides hanging out) but he was always still surprised at the range of nostril-scorching odours that a group of monsters could create. And that was just from the food.

"There's the toffee-frogsicle stand!" said Barry, pointing delightedly at a jolly monster who was standing at a table with a colourful umbrella. "Look at that great big tub of swamp toffee! It's the stickiest substance known to monsters, not to mention the most delicious."

"Plopcorn too - my favourite!" said Twig.

"And candy moss! Yummy! And Betty the beetle

can use it to make a little nest for herself as

well." A small black beetle appeared from a

woodworm hole in Twig's head and hopped

about excitedly.

They parked the Fuzzbuggy right in the

centre of the fairground. Then Fuzzby opened

the hatch in the side of the van. Almost

immediately there was a queue of monsters

waiting. Fuzzby's cooking was well known

across Monsterworld, especially his chips, and everyone seemed to be very hungry.

Fuzzby got to work in the kitchen, while Joe, Twig and Barry served the customers. They were kept very busy. It was just like being back in the diner, with lots of monsters keen to get their hands, claws or tentacles on Fuzzby's famous chips!

"Having fun must be good for the appetite," said Barry, raising his voice so Fuzzby could hear. "Maybe we'll get a turn soon..."

"We can take a break and explore later," said Fuzzby, fishing Betty the beetle out of a dollop of curry sauce. "First there's work to be done!"

Lots of customers were also friends of Fuzzby and the others, and had come to say hello. A small forest of young trees temporarily took root nearby. They were tree-monster friends of Twig who had heard all about Joe and wanted to see what her hooman boyfriend was like. They whispered together and giggled in a way that Joe found very embarrassing.

Fuzzby's cousin Zuffby also popped by to say hello. He was pushing a wheelbarrow.

"I'm going to stand under the Big Squeal," he explained, "and collect some free sandwich filling. It falls out of the sky around there."

There was only one monster who stopped

by to say hello that wasn't so welcome. He

slithered up to the Fuzzbuggy, shoving the

other monsters out of the way. Joe heard

a low HISSSSSS! close to his ear and knew

immediately who it was.

the monster said, with a nasty chuckle.

"Uncton Slugglesbutt!" said Joe. "Nice to

see you, I DON'T think!" Joe tried not to sound

scared, but Uncton Slugglesbutt was a right

villain. He was a rival cook and had crossed

paths with Joe and Fuzzby a couple of times

before, trying to ruin Fuzzby's reputation for

good food. He had even

threatened to put Joe

in a stew one day.

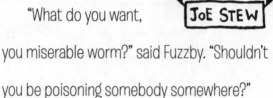

"What do you want,

you miserable worm?" said Fuzzby. "Shouldn't

you be poisoning somebody somewhere?"

"Charming!" said Uncton, pretending to be

offended. "I only wanted to say hello to you and

your pet." He patted Joe on the head as if he

was a dog. "I'm just here for the fun of the fair,"
Uncton continued. "No cooking for me today.
Not that I'd want to make food in the back of
a van in the middle of a field, anyway. I'm far
too important for that. Have a lovely day," he
said with a revolting smile as he wandered off
through the crowd.

"What's he up to?" said Fuzzby suspiciously.

"No good, that's for sure," said Joe.

"Maybe he's changed," suggested Twig.

"I think that's very unlikely," said Fuzzby.
"Uncton's a bad one, through and through."

Eventually, after working hard all morning,
Fuzzby suggested they shut up shop for a bit

and have a look around. Everyone cheered as

he closed the Fuzzbuggy's hatch and they set

off to explore.

They soon bumped

into some of the diner's

regulars. Bradwell had

knitted a trampoline for

the smaller monsters to

bounce around on. The

Guzzelins were merrily

leaping about on it, jumping

in formation and cheering

every time little Lemmy

Guzzelin did a somersault.

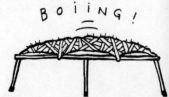

Next was Mr Jubbins's stall, where he was running a Guess What I've Just Eaten! competition. You had to look through his great big transparent jelly tummy and try to guess from all the swirling, half-digested food what Mr Jubbins had consumed for his last meal. One clever monster had written 'Everything' on his entry form, which was fairly accurate in Mr Jubbins's case, but fish-paste sandwiches were definitely off the menu after last year's unfortunate farting incident!

"Which rides shall we try?" said Joe.

He saw a sign saying **THIS WAY TO SPLODGEM DODGEMS** ⇒.

"What are they?" he asked.

"You drive around in the dodgem, bumping into tubs of frog custard and yak mucous," said Barry. "If you're really good at steering you can usually hit all of them and get covered in the stuff. Delicious!"

Joe didn't look convinced.

"Let's find something really scary!" said Twig. "A roller toaster, or... oooh, look!" She pointed to a sign that said TUNNEL OF TERROR. "That sounds perfect!" she exclaimed with worrying enthusiasm.

Underneath the sign was a small railway

track with little carriages sitting on it, waiting

for any passengers who felt brave enough

to have a go. Standing next to the train was

their old friend Petrolla. She was the monster

mechanic and inventor who had built the

Fuzzbuggy.

"ROLL UP, ROLL UP!" she roared at passers-

by. "Face your worst nightmares! Face your

deepest fears! The most frightening things a

monster could ever imagine! Dare you enter

the ⌈TUNNEL-OF⌉ ⌊TERROR⌋?" Petrolla bared her

teeth and growled for effect.

"Oh, hello, you lot," she said when she saw

them, suddenly changing back into the usual

round and friendly Petrolla. "Fancy a trip in the

Tunnel of Terror? I constructed it myself."

"That's terrifying enough," said Barry. "No,

thank you very much!" Petrolla's inventions

were famous for being rather unpredictable.

As far as she was concerned, a machine wasn't

a proper machine until it had crashed, caught

fire or exploded at least once, and preferably

all three.

"Come on," said Fuzzby. "We'll have a go. In you get, Barry."

Joe gulped. A Tunnel of Terror for monsters? What could possibly frighten them? He had once been on a ghost train at an amusement park at the seaside and it had scared him silly. He wasn't sure he could face this. But before he knew it, Fuzzby had picked him up and bundled him into a seat on the little train. When they were all in, Petrolla pressed a button and they slowly started moving.

"Off you go to your doom!" she said cheerily. "Have fun!"

"Wheeeeeee!" cried Twig, as the little train

headed towards a painted wooden tunnel. She

didn't look terrified at all. Joe clung to his seat.

What was going to happen?

Before they had even reached the tunnel, a

huge furry monster with enormous fangs

came charging towards them from out of the darkness! It bellowed with a horribly rough and throaty noise.

ARRRGGGHHH!! yelled Joe, almost jumping up in the air. This was a fine start!

"Don't go in there, it's petrifying! I'm getting out of here..." said the monster, running back the way they had just come from. Joe realised this wasn't part of the ride – just a terrified customer!

The ride must be really scary! thought Joe with a gulp. But it was too late to turn back as they sped into the blackness of the tunnel.

Everything was dark for a second, then a pair of yellow eyes suddenly appeared... A pair of yellow eyes that belonged to... a tiny, very cute, fluffy kitten.

"Meowww!" it said, in a high-pitched voice.

"AAIIEEEEEEEEEEEE!" the monsters screamed together. "Ohhhh, it's horrible, HORRIBLE!"

Joe looked confused. "It's just a kitten!"

he said, looking at the terrified monsters and

scratching his head.

Next up was a sweet, squishy teddy bear.

It gave a soft, mechanical growl.

"NOOOOOOOOOO!" screamed the monsters

again. "Make it go AWAY!" Barry cowered in

fear behind Fuzzby, covering each of his eyes with a tentacle. Meanwhile, Fuzzby chomped nervously on his claws and Twig was shaking so much that she was soon sitting in a compost heap made from the leaves that had fallen from her head.

"It's just a teddy bear," said Joe, chuckling at his friends. This was not what he had in mind as a scary ride at all!

Next came a giggling baby, then a vase of lovely flowers, then a little puppy with a pink bow round its neck.

"AAIIEEEEEEEEEEEE! AAIIEEEEEEEEEEEE! AAIIEEEEEEEEEEEE!" shrieked the monsters, clinging to each other in fear.

"You're so brave, Joe!" said Fuzzby, wiping the sweat from his brow.

"You monsters are so silly!" said Joe. "There's nothing to be afraid o-

ARRRGGGHHH!!"

Hee Hee!

A giant spider dropped from the ceiling,
its hairy legs waggling creepily. Joe and the
monsters all screamed together. Joe had
forgotten that monsters were petrified of
spiders, and even he was scared when they

were this big!

Double AAAARRRGGH!!

At last the train emerged again into daylight and trundled back to the start. Petrolla was pleased when her customers admitted that the Tunnel of Terror had lived up to its name.

"There was going to be a cute doll as well," she said, "but there was an explosion-related incident earlier today and all that's left is a pile of melted plastic."

"Probably for the best. I don't think we could have taken much more," said Fuzzby, shivering at the thought of all the hideous cuteness. "We'd better get back to the Fuzzbuggy. We've still got lots more food to sell."

"I fancy some chips myself," said Petrolla. "I'll come too."

They walked back to where they'd left the van. But when they got back there, there was only a bare patch of grass and no sign of the Fuzzbuggy at all. They looked around, puzzled.

"Where is it?" said Twig.

"I'm sure it was here," said Fuzzby in bewilderment. "Or has the Tunnel of Terror upset me so much that my brain has gone pink and fluffy too?"

"Look!" said Joe, pointing to the ground.

"Tyre tracks! The Fuzzbuggy was here. Someone

has driven off with it!"

"Clever lad," said Fuzzby. "Let's follow the

tracks and see where they lead."

The trail left by the Fuzzbuggy wove its way

through the fair. At first, it was easy to work

out the direction in which the van had gone, but after a while the tracks became more difficult to see.

"There are so many monsters trampling around that they've messed up the trail," said Petrolla.

Fuzzby was very upset. "My beautiful Fuzzbuggy!" he said. "I'll never see it again!"

Then Joe spotted something. An odd-looking monster was wandering past him, happily munching away on a biscuit. It was one of Barry's cat-cookies!

"Excuse me!" said Joe politely. "Where did you get that cookie from?"

"From that food tent over there," said the monster, pointing a tentacle towards a big white tent that stood next to the Splodgem Dodgems. "And it's one of the tastiest cookies I've ever eaten, or my name's not Sluggybottom Ninjapants... which it is!" The monster plodded away.

"Someone else is selling cat-cookies too!" said Barry. "What a coincidence. They looked almost as good as mine."

"They *were* yours, silly!" said Twig.

"I think we need to investigate this food tent," said Joe. "There's something funny going on."

A queue of monsters snaked past the dodgems and up to the tent's entrance. There was a handwritten sign hanging over it that said . Monsters were leaving with burgers and cakes and eating hungrily.

"Slugglesbutt Snacks?" said Fuzzby. "I

thought Uncton said he wasn't cooking at the fair!"

But sure enough, there was the nasty worm monster with an apron on, serving food through a flap in the tent. He saw Joe and the others coming towards him and, for a moment, Joe thought he looked worried. But Uncton soon recovered his usual sneer.

"Hello, again, Fuzzby, my dear friend," he said. "Would you care for a burger bite? Or a dead-and-buttered pudding?"

"What's going on?" said Fuzzby. "Why are you serving the same food as me?"

"It seemed like a good idea after all," said

Uncton smoothly. "I'm sure you can stand a bit

 of competition."

But it was obvious to Joe what was going on. This wasn't a food tent, it was the Fuzzbuggy disguised as a tent. Uncton had stolen it!

"You're selling Fuzzby's food!" said Joe. "Give us back the Fuzzbuggy, you slimy old worm! I know it's hidden under there!"

"Galloping grumblebugs!" exclaimed Fuzzby. "Joe, you're a genius! Hand over my Fuzzbuggy this instant, Slugglesbutt!" The big green monster growled and marched purposefully towards Uncton. But the worm wasn't going to wait to find out what Fuzzby would do. He darted to the front of the camouflaged

Fuzzbuggy and started the engine. A second later, the van roared off, the great big tent still attached and flapping in the breeze.

"We'll never catch him," gasped Twig. "It's too fast!"

"The dodgems!" said Fuzzby. "Quick! Jump in!"

Fuzzby, Joe, Barry and Twig squeezed into one of the empty dodgems.

"I'll give you a hand," said Petrolla (who actually had four hands, so it wasn't too difficult). She quickly opened the front of the dodgem and poked around inside with one of her special screwdrivers. Sparks flew out of the engine and it juddered into life.

"What have you done?" said Barry suspiciously. "Is there going to be an explosion?"

Petrolla laughed. "Let's just say I've given this dodgem a little power boost," she said. "You shouldn't have any trouble catching him now. Now go!"

Fuzzby pressed one of his big feet hard on the pedal and the dodgem whizzed off the ride like a rocket, knocking over several tubs of mucous and custard on the way. The little dodgem was fast as lightning, and was soon on the tail of the tent-buggy as it sped ahead of

Wait for us!

them through the fairground. Uncton was not

used to driving a van, so it bounced around the

field haphazardly. Zigzagging in all directions,

it collided with other tents and food stalls,

sending monsters running all over the place.

AWOOOGAH! Uncton sounded the Fuzzbuggy's

horn furiously.

"Get out of the way, you idiot!" he cried as

he knocked Zuffby's wheelbarrow flying.

"I spent two hours standing under the Big Squeal collecting that sandwich filling!" shouted an angry Zuffby, shaking a fist at the Fuzzbuggy as it zoomed off. The contents

of his wheelbarrow splattered all over the Fuzzbuggy's windscreen. Uncton switched on the windscreen wipers, drenching a nearby family of bobble-beasts in cold sick.

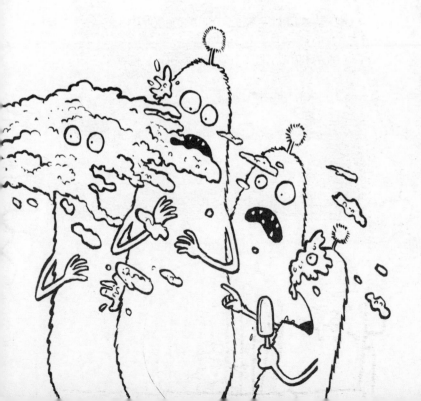

"We've almost caught up with it!" yelled Barry, who was hanging on to Fuzzby's head for dear life. "What do we do now?"

"We can climb in through the hatch," screeched Twig, "and try to take control of the van from Uncton."

"I'm not climbing through there!" protested Barry, watching the ground speeding past below him. "That's too much of a sticky situation for my liking!"

A sticky situation? That gave Joe an idea...

"Drive the dodgem alongside the van, Fuzzby!" he shouted.

Fuzzby carefully steered the dodgem until

they were level with Uncton in the front of the

Fuzzbuggy. The worm leant out of the window

and hissed at them.

"You can't catch me!" he cackled. "I could

easily squash you in that little thing!" It was

exactly what Joe was hoping he would say.

That Uncton
is pure evil!

I'm appalled!

"You're right!" Joe said. "You could flatten us all with the Fuzzbuggy. Just think, you'd be rid of your rival chef and a bothersome hooman all in one go."

"What are you doing?" yelled Barry in disbelief. "Don't tell him that!"

But an evil glint had appeared in Uncton's eye. He suddenly pulled on the van's steering wheel, and the Fuzzbuggy swerved towards the dodgem. Fuzzby just managed to steer the little car away in time.

"He's trying to run us over!" said Twig in horror.

"We're all going to die!" cried Barry. "I've got

so much to give to the
world. I can't die now!"

"I'm hoping you
have something in
mind..." said Fuzzby to Joe.

"We want him to follow
us," explained Joe. "Head back to the toffee-
frogsicle stall!"

Fuzzby steered the dodgem back towards
the fair.

"It worked! He's following!" said Twig,
looking around. "And gaining ground! He
definitely wants to squish us!"

The Fuzzbuggy chased the little dodgem

through the fair, the two strange-looking

vehicles weaving dangerously in and out of all

the rides and stalls.

"Watch out for the candy-moss stand!"

Joe warned. But it was too late. The dodgem

ploughed straight through it. Sticky moss

flew up into the air and covered Joe and the

monsters so they all looked like they had

sprouted tufts of green hair. Betty the beetle

couldn't believe her luck.

"Sorry!" Fuzzby called to the surprised

candy-moss monster. "We'll pay later!"

"Make sure you don't hit the toffee-

frogsicle stall as well!" said Twig, brushing moss

off her face.

With a sudden turn of the wheel, Fuzzby steered the dodgem past the stall.

"Here, give us a hand, Barry," said Joe, reaching over for the tub of sticky swamp toffee as they drove past.

"A snack, what a good idea!" said Barry, helping Joe grab it.

"It's not for eating!" said Joe.

The Fuzzbuggy was right behind them now, the tent still wrapped around it. Soon it was so close it almost touched the dodgem. Uncton cackled evilly once more.

"He's going to get us!" wailed Twig, covering her eyes.

"Not if I can help it!" said Joe.

Just when it looked like they were about to get squashed, Joe leant over the side of the dodgem and poured the sticky toffee over the ground. The Fuzzbuggy drove straight into the pool of gluey brown liquid, its wheels sticking to the toffee.

"What have you done, you stupid hooman!" shouted Uncton angrily, slamming a fist on the steering wheel.

But it was no use. The swamp toffee had hardened like cement and the wheels were stuck.

Uncton tried to make a dash for it, but as he burst through the door, he got caught up in the material of the tent. He thrashed around in fury, but only got himself more entangled. He hissed and trembled in rage as the dodgem casually drew up alongside him, carefully avoiding the toffee.

"Curse you, hooman!" he said to Joe. "Next time we meet, it'll be the stew pot for you!"

"It might be some time before that happens," said Fuzzby with a growl. "Someone call the Monsterworld police! They might have something to say about your thievery."

Uncton sagged in his tent cocoon like an unhappy caterpillar.

"Bah!" he said.

"Well done, you hero!" said Twig, giving Joe a hug as her tree-monster friends watched and giggled. Joe blushed.

"You're a marvel, Joe!" said Fuzzby, picking him up for another monster hug. "I thought we were in trouble for a moment!"

"Me too," said Joe. "I'm just glad we got the Fuzzbuggy back in one piece!"

"It looks like it will need a good wash. AGAIN," muttered Barry, surveying the toffee-plastered van. "I can lick it clean this time, though," he added. "I love a bit of swamp toffee. Yum!"

Fuzzby wasn't bothered by the mess, he was just so happy to have his Fuzzbuggy back. The big green monster opened the van door and climbed into the kitchen.

"Before there's any cleaning, we need to thank the hero of the day," he said. "Joe Shoe! Why don't I make us something to celebrate.

We love a happy ending!

What do you fancy, Joe?"

"Chips, of course!" said Joe, beaming. "And make sure they're MONSTER-sized!"

More monster-sized fun

DAVID O'CONNELL

MONSTER and CHIPS

Where the food bites back...

Hungry for more?

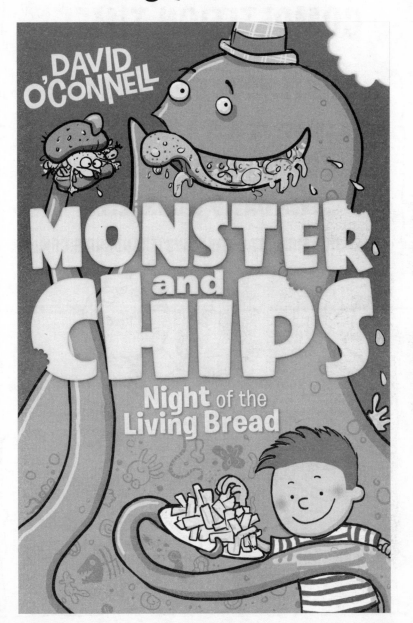

ToDAY'S SPECIALS

**Fill your belly today at
www.monsterandchips.com**

UH OH!

* **Creepy Competitions** (AND CHiPS)

* **Disturbing Downloads** (AND CHiPS)

* **Slimy Sneak Peeks** (AND CHiPS)

* **Revolting Reviews** (AND CHiPS)

FUZZBY'S
TRY OUR FAMOUS CHiPS!

MY FAVOURITE!

Got a taste for great stories?
Why not tuck into these other
great books from HarperCollins:

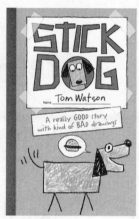

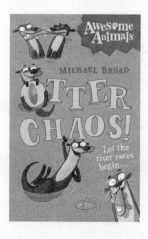